This igloo book belongs to:

Eilidh Thompson

igloobooks

Published in 2020
First published in the UK by Igloo Books Ltd
An imprint of Igloo Books Ltd
Cottage Farm, NN6 0BJ, UK
Owned by Bonnier Books
Sveavägen 56, Stockholm, Sweden
www.igloobooks.com

1020 002
2 4 6 8 10 9 7 5 3
ISBN 978-1-83852-216-2

Written by Stephanie Moss
Illustrated by Louise Forshaw

Designed by Hannah George
Edited by Hannah Campling

Printed and manufactured in China

GREAT

fairies

OF THE WORLD

igloobooks

Fairyland's somewhere we'd all like to go.
But there is something that you might not know.

Swishing their wands isn't all fairies do.

They're brave and they're clever, and so much more, too!

Remember their fairy dust,
shimmering pink.
Where does it all come from,
did you ever think?

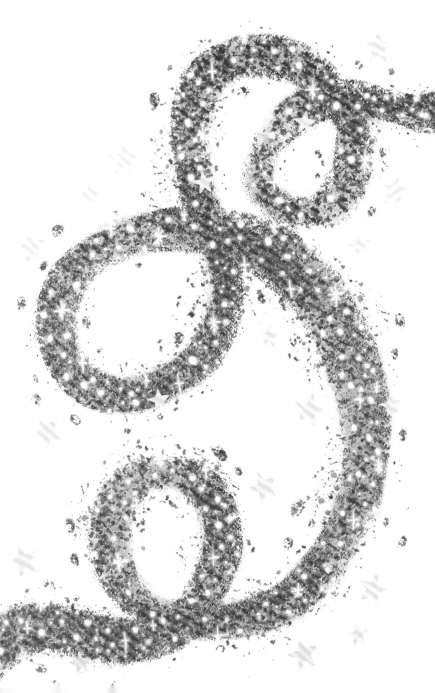

The scientist fairies
work into the night,
till the formula's perfect
and **glittering** bright!

Once fairies have dust, they all need a wand, too.
Inventors make those, and one day, so could you!

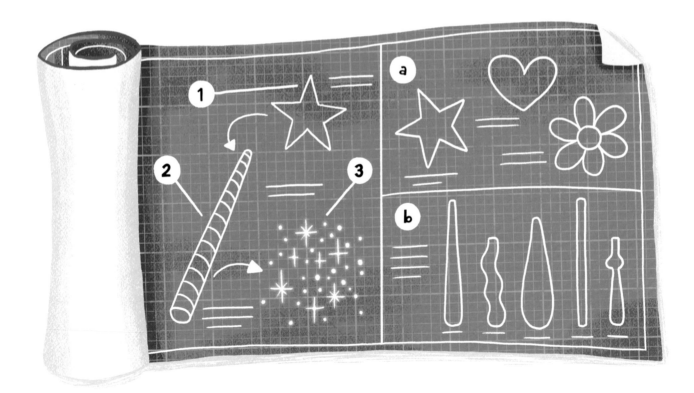

They draw up their plans and they study all day.

Soon the wands work. **Hooray!**

Now, look at the houses, down in Fairy Wood.
Who do you think makes them all look so good?

Meet Architect Fairy,
with her building crew.
They've got the right tools
and know just what to do.

If fairies feel ill or get hurt in a fall,
the kind doctor fairies are who they will call.

They've trained very hard and learned each healing spell
to make fairies better and keep them all well.

Of course, there are fairies who make flying cars.

They **whizz** above houses...

then **shoot** past the stars!

But engineer fairies are part of a team.
Mechanics make everything run like a **dream!**

Pet dragons **love** breathing fire in the air.
But if it goes wrong, the firefighters are there!

The **bravest** of fairies come to the rescue.
They put out hot flames, as the crowd cheers, **"Woo-hoo!"**

The vaults of the palace are **deep** underground, and that's where the counting fairies can be found.

They keep track of gold that's stacked up ten feet high,
by doing their sums in the **blink** of an eye.

And who do you think runs the **whole** magic town?
The fairy that does more than just wear a crown!

A queen must be strong and courageous, but kind.

The most INSPIRATIONAL fairy you'll find!

Remember that fairies are more than they seem.
They do more than **shimmer** and **glitter** and **gleam**.

They live in a land full of magic and spells, but they're **strong**, **brave** and **clever**...

... and **you** are, as well!

The Dragon Rescue
Shield for Bravery

Cosiest Toadstool
Architecture Prize

Inventor of
the Best Wand

The Gold Coin
Counting Prize

Most Inspirational
Fairy of All

Magical Healing
Award for Kindness

The Sparkliest
Dust Maker

Trophy for the
Fastest Flying Car

Enchanting
Engineering Prize